SCARY
FAIRY TALES

The Rat Catcher
and Other Stories

COMPILED BY VIC PARKER

 Gareth Stevens
PUBLISHING

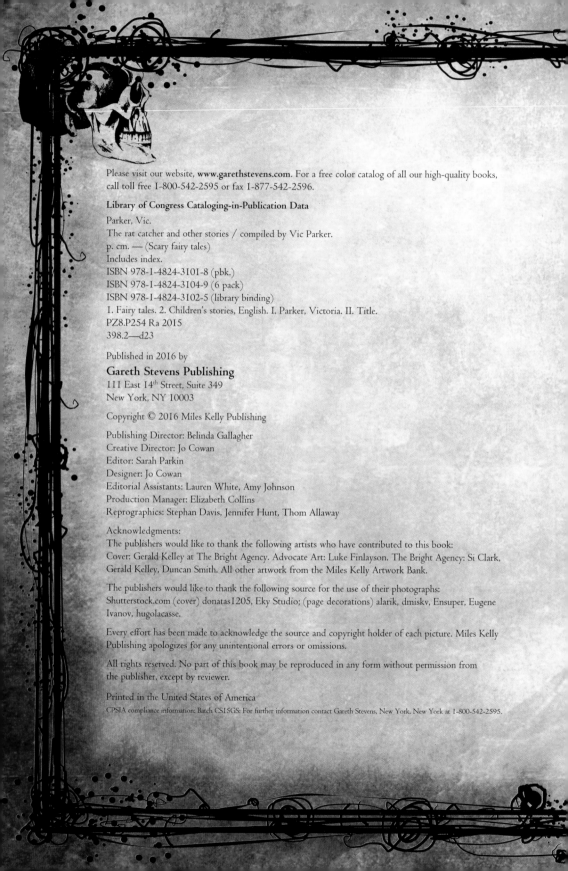

Please visit our website, **www.garethstevens.com**. For a free color catalog of all our high-quality books, call toll free 1-800-542-2595 or fax 1-877-542-2596.

Library of Congress Cataloging-in-Publication Data

Parker, Vic.
The rat catcher and other stories / compiled by Vic Parker.
p. cm. — (Scary fairy tales)
Includes index.
ISBN 978-1-4824-3101-8 (pbk.)
ISBN 978-1-4824-3104-9 (6 pack)
ISBN 978-1-4824-3102-5 (library binding)
1. Fairy tales. 2. Children's stories, English. I. Parker, Victoria. II. Title.
PZ8.P254 Ra 2015
398.2—d23

Published in 2016 by

Gareth Stevens Publishing
111 East 14th Street, Suite 349
New York, NY 10003

Publishing Director: Belinda Gallagher
Creative Director: Jo Cowan
Editor: Sarah Parkin
Designer: Jo Cowan
Editorial Assistants: Lauren White, Amy Johnson
Production Manager: Elizabeth Collins
Reprographics: Stephan Davis, Jennifer Hunt, Thom Allaway

Acknowledgments:
The publishers would like to thank the following artists who have contributed to this book:
Cover: Gerald Kelley at The Bright Agency. Advocate Art: Luke Finlayson. The Bright Agency: Si Clark, Gerald Kelley, Duncan Smith. All other artwork from the Miles Kelly Artwork Bank.

The publishers would like to thank the following source for the use of their photographs:
Shutterstock.com (cover) donatas1205, Eky Studio; (page decorations) alarik, dmiskv, Ensuper, Eugene Ivanov, hugolacasse.

Every effort has been made to acknowledge the source and copyright holder of each picture. Miles Kelly Publishing apologizes for any unintentional errors or omissions.

Printed in the United States of America

CPSIA compliance information: Batch CS15GS: For further information contact Gareth Stevens, New York, New York at 1-800-542-2595.

Contents

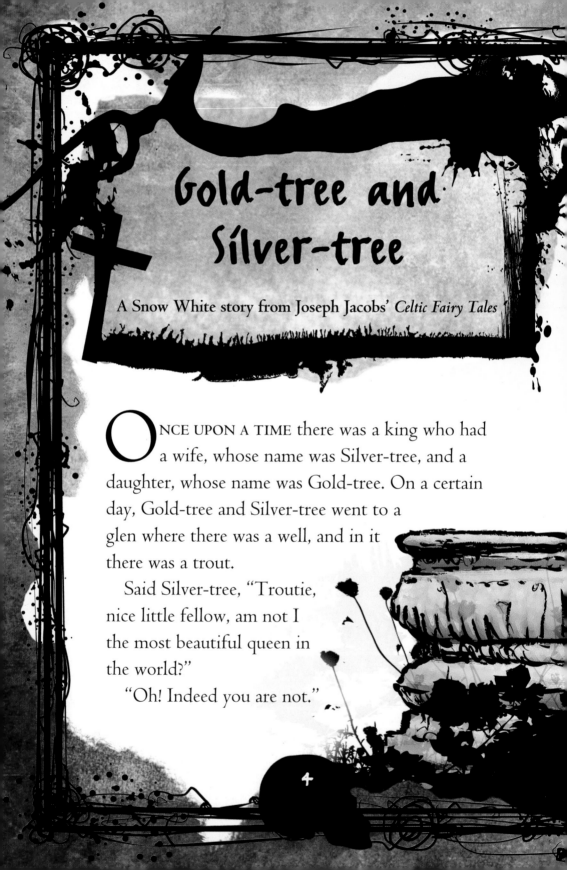

Gold-tree and Silver-tree

A Snow White story from Joseph Jacobs' *Celtic Fairy Tales*

Once upon a time there was a king who had a wife, whose name was Silver-tree, and a daughter, whose name was Gold-tree. On a certain day, Gold-tree and Silver-tree went to a glen where there was a well, and in it there was a trout.

Said Silver-tree, "Troutie, nice little fellow, am not I the most beautiful queen in the world?"

"Oh! Indeed you are not."

"Who then?"

"Why, Gold-tree, your daughter."

Silver-tree went home, blind with rage. She lay down on the bed, and vowed she would never be well until she could get the heart and the liver of Gold-tree, her daughter, to eat.

At nightfall the king came home, and it was told to him that Silver-tree, his wife, was very ill. He went where she was, and asked her what was wrong.

"Oh! Only a thing which you may heal if you like."

"Oh! Indeed there is nothing at all which I could do for you that I would not do."

"If I get the

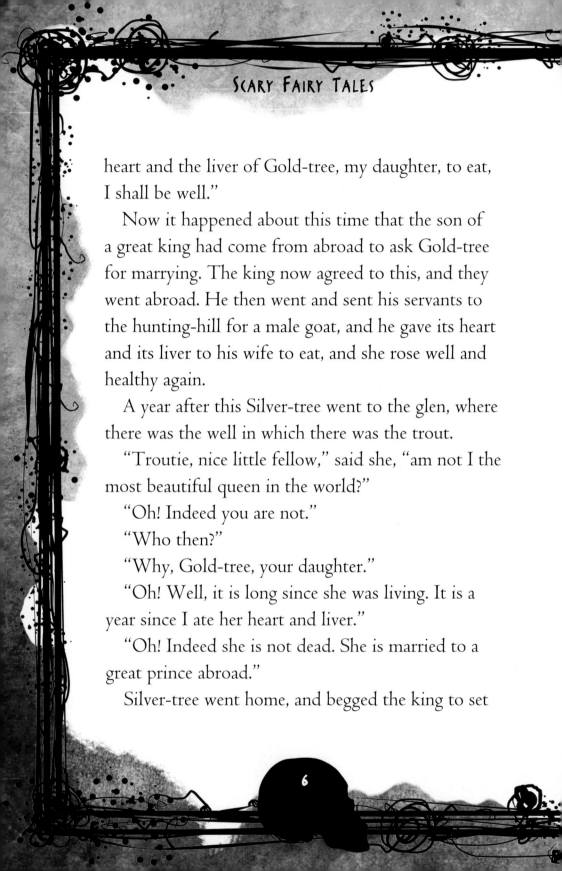

heart and the liver of Gold-tree, my daughter, to eat, I shall be well."

Now it happened about this time that the son of a great king had come from abroad to ask Gold-tree for marrying. The king now agreed to this, and they went abroad. He then went and sent his servants to the hunting-hill for a male goat, and he gave its heart and its liver to his wife to eat, and she rose well and healthy again.

A year after this Silver-tree went to the glen, where there was the well in which there was the trout.

"Troutie, nice little fellow," said she, "am not I the most beautiful queen in the world?"

"Oh! Indeed you are not."

"Who then?"

"Why, Gold-tree, your daughter."

"Oh! Well, it is long since she was living. It is a year since I ate her heart and liver."

"Oh! Indeed she is not dead. She is married to a great prince abroad."

Silver-tree went home, and begged the king to set

the longboat ready, and said, "I am going to see my dear Gold-tree, for it is so long since I saw her."

The longboat was ready, and they went away.

It was Silver-tree herself that was at the helm, and she steered the ship so well that it was not long at all before they arrived.

The prince was out hunting on the hills. Gold-tree knew her father's longboat was coming.

"Oh!" said she to the servants. "My mother is coming, and she will kill me."

"She shall not kill you at all; we will lock you in a room where she cannot get near you."

This is how it was done; and when Silver-tree came ashore, she began to cry out: "Come to meet your own mother, when she comes to see you."

Gold-tree said that she

could not, that she was locked in the room, and that she could not get out of it.

"Will you not put your little finger through the keyhole," said Silver-tree "so that your own mother may give a kiss to it?"

She put out her little finger, and Silver-tree went and stuck a poisoned needle in it, and Gold-tree fell dead.

When the prince came home, and found Gold-tree dead, he was in great sorrow, and when he saw how beautiful she was, he did not bury her, but he locked her in a room where nobody would get near her.

In the course of time he married again, and the whole house was under the hand of this wife but one room, and he always kept the key of that room to himself. On a certain day he forgot to take the key with him, and the second wife got into the room. What did she see there but the most beautiful woman that she ever saw.

She began to try to wake her, and she noticed the poisoned needle in her finger. She took the needle out, and Gold-tree rose alive, as beautiful as she was ever.

At the fall of night the prince came home from the hunting-hill, looking very downcast.

"What gift," said his wife, "would you give me if I could make you laugh?"

"Oh! Indeed, nothing could make me laugh, except Gold-tree were to come alive again."

"Well, you'll find her alive in the room."

When the prince saw Gold-tree alive he made great rejoicings, and he began to kiss her and kiss her.

Said the second wife to the prince, "Since she is the first one you had it is better for you to stick to her, and I will go away."

"Oh! Indeed you shall not go away, but I shall have both of you."

At the end of the year, Silver-tree went to the glen, where there was the well, in which there was the trout. "Troutie, nice little fellow," said she, "am not I the most beautiful queen in the world?"

"Oh! Indeed you are not."

"Who then?"

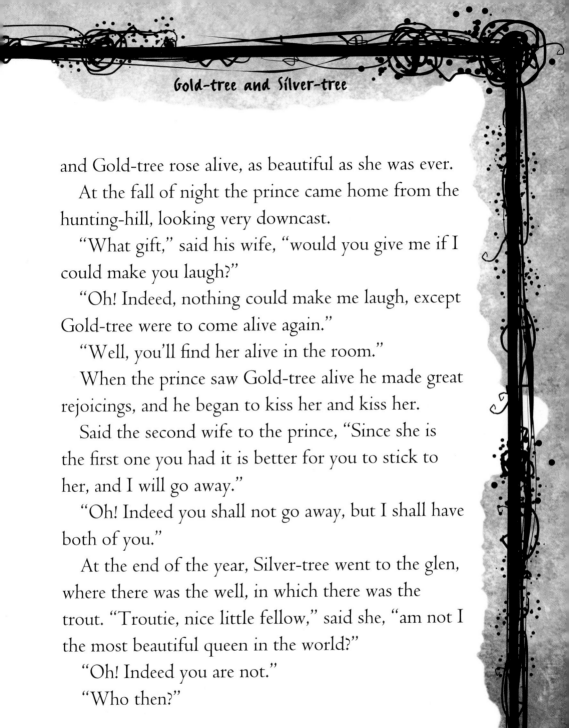

"Why, Gold-tree, your daughter."

"Oh! Well, she is not alive. It is a year since I put the poisoned needle into her finger."

"Oh! Indeed she is not dead at all."

Silver-tree went home, and begged the king to get the longboat ready, for she was going to see her dear Gold-tree, as it was so long since she saw her. The longboat was ready, and they went away. It was Silver-tree herself that was at the helm, and she steered the ship so well that they were not long at all before they arrived.

The prince was out hunting on the hills. Gold-tree knew her father's ship coming.

"Oh!" said she. "My mother is coming, and she will kill me."

"Not at all," said the second wife; "we will go down to meet her."

Silver-tree came ashore. "Come down, Gold-tree, love," said she, "for your own mother has come to you with a precious drink." Of course, the wicked woman had laced it with poison.

"It is a custom in this country," said the second wife, "that the person who offers a drink takes a sip out of it first."

Silver-tree put her mouth to it, and the second wife went and struck it so that some of it went down her throat, and she fell dead. They had only to carry her home a dead corpse and bury her.

The prince and his two wives were long alive after this, pleased and peaceful.

The Rat Catcher

From Andrew Lang's *Red Fairy Book*

A VERY LONG TIME AGO the town of Hamel in Germany was invaded by bands of rats, the likes of which had never been seen before nor will ever be seen again.

They were great black creatures that ran boldly in broad daylight through the streets, and swarmed all over the houses, so that people could not put their hand or foot down anywhere without touching one. When dressing in the morning they found them in their pants and purses, in their pockets and in their boots; and when they wanted a morsel to eat, the voracious horde had swept away everything from cellar to attic. The night was even worse. As soon as the lights were out, these untiring nibblers set to work. And everywhere, in the ceilings, in the floors, in the cupboards, at the doors, there was a chase and a rummage, and so furious a noise, that a deaf man

could not have rested for one hour together.

Neither cats nor dogs, nor poison nor traps, nor prayers nor candles burned to all the saints – nothing would do anything. The more they killed the more came. And the inhabitants of Hamel began to go to the dogs (not that *they* were of much use), when one Friday there arrived in the town a man who played the bagpipes and sang this refrain:

> "*Qui vivra verra:*
> *Le voila,*
> *Le preneur des rats.*"

He was a great gawky fellow, dry and bronzed, with a crooked nose, a long rat-tail mustache, two great yellow eyes, under a large felt hat set off by a scarlet rooster feather. He was dressed in a green jacket with a leather belt and red pants, and on his feet were sandals fastened by thongs passed around his legs. That is how he may be seen to this day, painted on a window of the cathedral of Hamel.

He stopped on the great marketplace before the town hall, turned his back to the church and went on with his music, singing:

> "Who lives shall see:
> This is he,
> The rat catcher."

The town council had just assembled to consider once more this plague, from which no one could save the town. The stranger sent word to the counselors that, if they would make it worth his while, he would rid them of all their rats before night, down to the very last one.

"Then he is a sorcerer!" cried the citizens with one voice. "We must beware of him."

The Town Counselor, who was considered clever, reassured them.

He said: "Sorcerer or not, if this bagpiper speaks the truth, it was he who sent us this horrible vermin that he wants to rid us of today for money. Well, we must learn to catch the Devil in his own snares. You leave it to me."

"Leave it to the Town Counselor," said the citizens one to another.

And the stranger was brought before them.

"Before night," said the stranger, "I shall have dispatched all the rats in Hamel if you will but pay me one coin per head."

"A coin per head!" cried the citizens. "But that will come to millions of coins!"

The Town Counselor simply shrugged his shoulders and said to the stranger: "A bargain! To work; the rats will be paid one coin per head."

The bagpiper announced that he would operate that very evening when the moon rose. He added that the inhabitants should at that hour leave the streets free, and content themselves with looking out of their windows at what was passing, and that it would be a pleasant spectacle.

When the people of Hamel heard of the bargain, they too exclaimed: "A coin per head! But this will cost us a great deal of money!"

"Leave it to the Town Counselor," said the town council with a malicious air. And the good people of Hamel repeated with their counselors, "Leave it to the Town Counselor."

Towards nine at night the bagpiper reappeared on the marketplace. He turned, as at first, his back on the church, and the moment the moon rose on the horizon, "Trarira, trari!" the bagpipes resounded.

It was first a slow, caressing sound, then more and more lively and urgent, and so sonorous and piercing that it penetrated as far as the farthest alleys and retreats of the town.

Soon from the bottom of the cellars, the top of the attics, from under all the furniture, from all the nooks and corners of the houses, out came the rats, searching for the door, flinging themselves into the street, and trip, trip, trip, began to run in file towards the front of the town hall, so squeezed together that they covered the pavement like waves.

When the square was all full the bagpiper looked around, and, still playing briskly, turned towards the river that runs at the foot of the walls of Hamel.

When he arrived there he turned around; the rats were following.

"Hop! Hop!" he cried, pointing with his finger to the middle of the stream, where the water whirled and was drawn down as if through a funnel. And hop! Hop! Without hesitating, the rats took the leap, swam straight to the funnel, plunged in head foremost and disappeared.

The plunging continued till midnight.

At last, dragging himself with difficulty, came a big rat, white with age, and it stopped on the bank.

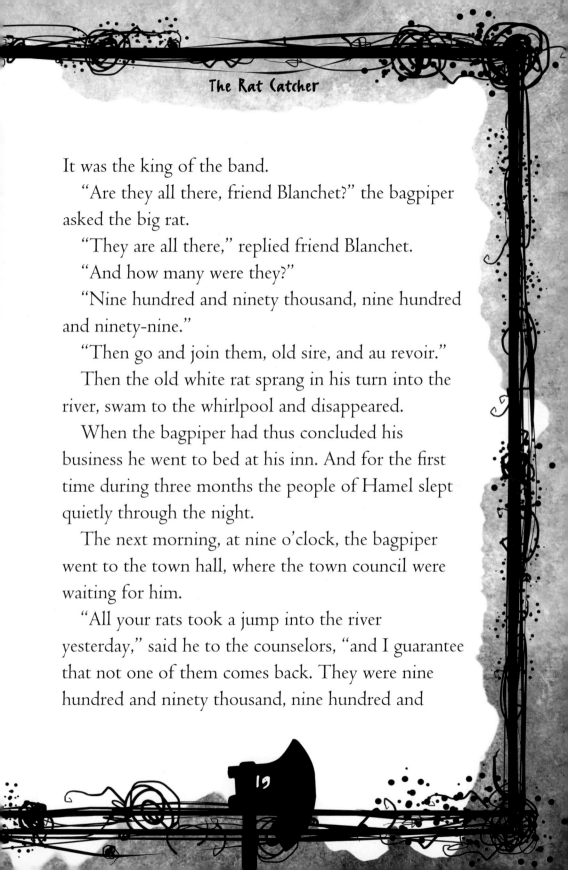

It was the king of the band.

"Are they all there, friend Blanchet?" the bagpiper asked the big rat.

"They are all there," replied friend Blanchet.

"And how many were they?"

"Nine hundred and ninety thousand, nine hundred and ninety-nine."

"Then go and join them, old sire, and au revoir."

Then the old white rat sprang in his turn into the river, swam to the whirlpool and disappeared.

When the bagpiper had thus concluded his business he went to bed at his inn. And for the first time during three months the people of Hamel slept quietly through the night.

The next morning, at nine o'clock, the bagpiper went to the town hall, where the town council were waiting for him.

"All your rats took a jump into the river yesterday," said he to the counselors, "and I guarantee that not one of them comes back. They were nine hundred and ninety thousand, nine hundred and

ninety-nine, at one coin a head. Reckon!"

"Let us reckon the heads first. One coin a head is one head per coin. Where are the heads?"

The rat catcher did not expect this treacherous stroke. He paled with anger and his eyes flashed fire. "The heads!" cried he. "If you care about them, go and find them in the river."

"So," replied the Town Counselor, "you refuse to hold to the terms of your agreement? We ourselves could refuse you all payment. But you have been of use to us, and we will not let you go without a recompense," and he offered him fifty crowns.

"Keep your recompense for yourself," replied the rat catcher proudly. "If you do not pay me I will be paid by your heirs."

Thereupon he pulled his hat down over his eyes, went hastily out of the hall, and left the town without speaking to a soul.

When the Hamel people heard how the affair had ended they rubbed their hands, and with no more scruple than their Town Counselor, they laughed

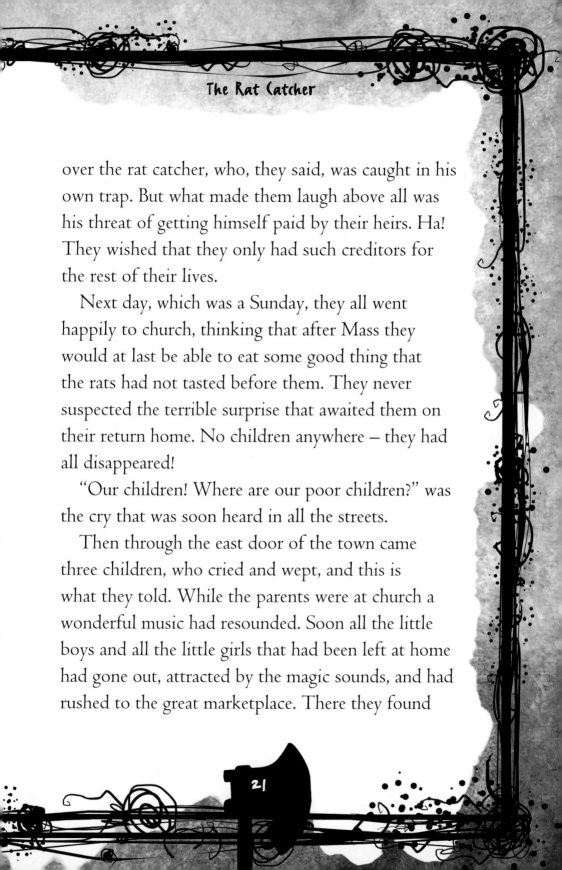

over the rat catcher, who, they said, was caught in his
own trap. But what made them laugh above all was
his threat of getting himself paid by their heirs. Ha!
They wished that they only had such creditors for
the rest of their lives.

Next day, which was a Sunday, they all went
happily to church, thinking that after Mass they
would at last be able to eat some good thing that
the rats had not tasted before them. They never
suspected the terrible surprise that awaited them on
their return home. No children anywhere – they had
all disappeared!

"Our children! Where are our poor children?" was
the cry that was soon heard in all the streets.

Then through the east door of the town came
three children, who cried and wept, and this is
what they told. While the parents were at church a
wonderful music had resounded. Soon all the little
boys and all the little girls that had been left at home
had gone out, attracted by the magic sounds, and had
rushed to the great marketplace. There they found

the rat catcher playing his bagpipes at the same spot as the evening before. Then the stranger had begun to walk quickly, and they had followed, running, singing and dancing to the sound of the music, as far as the foot of the mountain which one sees on entering Hamel. At their approach the mountain had opened a little, and the bagpiper and children had gone in, after which it had closed again. Only the three little ones who told the adventure had remained outside, as if by a miracle. One was bowlegged and could not run fast enough; the other, who had left the house in haste, wearing only one shoe, had hurt himself against a big stone and could not walk without difficulty; the third had arrived in time, but in hurrying to go in with the others, had struck so violently against the wall of the mountain that he fell backwards at the moment it closed.

At this story the parents redoubled their lamentations. They ran with pikes and mattocks to the mountain, and searched till

evening to find the opening in which their children had disappeared, without being able to find it. At last, the night falling, they returned desolate to Hamel.

But the most unhappy of all was the Town Counselor, for he lost three little boys and two pretty little girls, and to crown all, the people of Hamel overwhelmed him with reproaches, forgetting that the evening before they had all agreed with him.

What had become of all these children?

The parents always hoped they were not dead, and that the rat catcher, who certainly must have come out of the mountain, would have taken them with him to his country. That is why for several years they went in search of them to different countries, but no one ever came on the trace of the poor little ones.

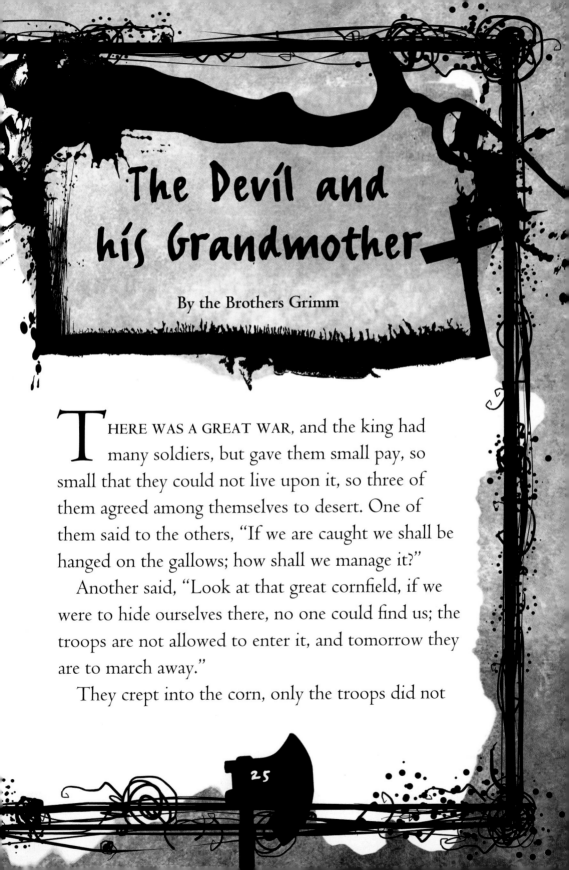

The Devil and his Grandmother

By the Brothers Grimm

THERE WAS A GREAT WAR, and the king had many soldiers, but gave them small pay, so small that they could not live upon it, so three of them agreed among themselves to desert. One of them said to the others, "If we are caught we shall be hanged on the gallows; how shall we manage it?"

Another said, "Look at that great cornfield, if we were to hide ourselves there, no one could find us; the troops are not allowed to enter it, and tomorrow they are to march away."

They crept into the corn, only the troops did not

march away, but remained lying all around it. They stayed in the corn for two days and two nights, and were so hungry that they all but died, but if they had come out, their death would have been certain. Then they said, "What is the use of our deserting if we have to perish miserably here?"

But now a fiery dragon came flying through the air, and it came down to them, and asked why they had hidden themselves there. They answered, "We are three soldiers who have deserted because the pay was so bad, and now we shall have to die of hunger if we stay here, or to dangle on the gallows if we go out."

"If you will serve me for seven years," said the dragon, "I will carry you through the army so that no one shall seize you."

"We have no choice, so we have to accept," the soldiers replied.

Then the dragon caught hold of them with his claws, and carried them away through the air over the army, and put them down again on the earth far from it; but the dragon was no other than the Devil.

He gave them a small whip and said, "Whip with it and crack it, and then as much gold will spring up around you as you can wish for; then you can live like great lords, keep horses, and drive your carriages, but when the seven years have come to an end, you are my property." Then he put in front of them a book which all three were forced to sign. "I will, however, then give you a riddle," said the dragon, "and if you can guess that, you shall be free, and released from my power."

Then the dragon flew away from them, and they went away with their whip, had gold aplenty, ordered themselves rich clothes, and traveled about the world.

Wherever they were they lived in pleasure and magnificence, rode on horseback, drove in carriages, ate and drank, but did nothing wicked.

The time slipped quickly away, and when the seven years were coming to an end, two of them were terribly anxious and alarmed; but the third took matters easily, and said, "Brothers, fear nothing, my head is sharp enough, I shall guess the riddle." They went out into the open country and sat down, and the two made sorrowful faces.

Then an aged woman came up to them who inquired why they were so sad.

"Alas!" they said. "How can that concern you? After all, you cannot help us."

"Who knows?" she replied. "Confide your trouble to me."

So they told her that they had been the Devil's servants for nearly seven years, and that he had provided them with gold as plentifully as if it had been blackberries, but that they had sold themselves to him, and were forfeited to him, if at the end of the seven years they could not guess a riddle.

The old woman said, "If you are to be saved, one of you must go into the forest, there he will come to a fallen rock which looks like a little house, he must enter that, and then he will obtain help."

The two melancholy ones thought to themselves, "That will still not save us," and stayed where they were, but the third, the merry one, got up and walked on in the forest until he found the rock-house.

In the little house, however, a very aged woman was sitting, who was the Devil's grandmother, and asked the soldier where he came from, and what he wanted there. He told her everything that had happened and, as he pleased her well, she had pity on him, and said she would help him. She lifted up a great stone which lay above a cellar, and said, "Hide yourself there, you can hear everything that is said here; only sit still, and do not stir. When the dragon comes, I will question him about the riddle. He tells everything to me, so listen carefully to his answer."

At twelve o'clock at night, the dragon came flying

there and asked for his dinner. The grandmother laid the table and served up food and drink, so that he was pleased, and they ate and drank together. In the course of conversation, she asked him what kind of a day he had had, and how many souls he had got?

"Nothing went very well today," he answered, "but I have laid hold of

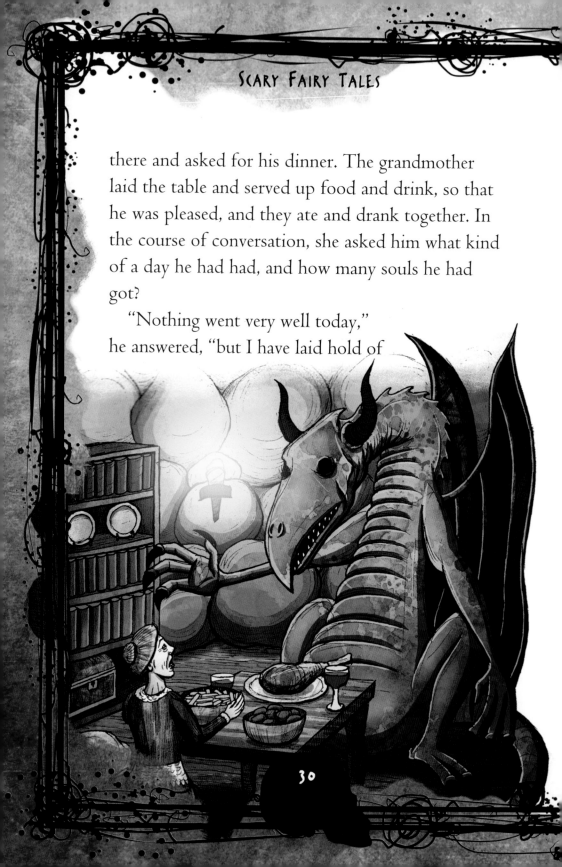

three soldiers, I have them safe."

"Indeed! Three soldiers, that's something good, but they may escape you yet."

The Devil said mockingly, "They are mine! I will set them a riddle, which they will never in this world be able to guess!"

"What riddle is that?" she inquired.

"I will tell you. In the great North Sea lies a dead dogfish, that shall be your roast meat, and the rib of a whale shall be your silver spoon, and a hollow old horse's hoof shall be your wine glass."

When the Devil had gone to bed, the grandmother raised up the stone and let out the soldier. "Did you pay careful attention to everything?" she asked.

"Yes," said he, "I know enough."

Then he went back to his companions. He told them how the Devil had been tricked by the old grandmother, and how he had learned the answer to the riddle from him. Then they were all joyous and of good cheer, and took the whip and whipped so much gold for themselves that it ran all over the ground.

When the seven years had fully gone by, the Devil came with the book, showed the signatures, and said, "I will take you with me to hell. There you shall have a meal. If you can guess what kind of roast meat you will have to eat, you shall be free and released from your bargain, and may keep the whip as well."

The first soldier said, "In the great North Sea lies a dead dogfish, that no doubt is the roast meat."

The Devil was angry, and began to mutter, "Hm! Hm! Hm!" And he asked the second, "But what will your spoon be?"

"The rib of a whale, that is to be our silver spoon."

The Devil made a wry face, again growled, "Hm! Hm! Hm!" and said to the third, "And do you also know what your wine glass is to be?"

"An old horse's hoof is to be our wine glass."

Then the Devil flew away with a loud cry, and had no more power over them, but the three kept the whip, whipped as much money for themselves with it as they wanted, and lived happily to their end.

The King who would see Paradise

From Andrew Lang's *Orange Fairy Book*

ONCE UPON A TIME there was a king who, one day out hunting, came upon a holy man, or fakeer, in a lonely place in the mountains. The fakeer was seated on a little old bedstead reading the Koran, with his patched cloak thrown over his shoulders.

The king asked him what he was reading; and he said he was reading about Paradise, and praying that he might be worthy to enter there. Then they began to talk, and the king asked the fakeer if he could show him a glimpse of Paradise, for he found it impossible to believe in what he could not see. The

fakeer replied that he was asking a very difficult, and
perhaps a very dangerous, thing; but that he would
pray for him, and perhaps he might be able to do it.
Only he warned the king both against the dangers
of his unbelief, and against the curiosity which
prompted him to ask this thing. However, the king
was not to be swayed, and he promised the fakeer
always to provide him with food, if he, in return,
would pray for him. To this the fakeer agreed, and so
they parted.

Time went on, and the king always sent the
old fakeer his food according to his promise; but,
whenever he sent to ask him when he was going to
show him Paradise, the fakeer always replied: "Not
yet, not yet!"

After a year or two had passed, the king heard one
day that the fakeer was very ill — indeed, believed
to be dying. Instantly he hurried off and found that
it was really true, and that the fakeer was even then
breathing his last breath. There and then the king
besought him to remember his promise, and to show

him a glimpse of Paradise. The dying fakeer replied that if the king would come to his funeral and, when the grave was filled in, and everyone else was gone away, he would come and lay his hand upon the grave, he would keep his word, and show him a glimpse of Paradise. At the same time he implored the king not to do this thing, but to be content to see Paradise when God called him there. Still the king's curiosity was so aroused that he would not give way.

Accordingly, after the fakeer was dead and had been buried, the king stayed behind when all the rest went away; and then, when he was quite alone, he stepped forward, and laid his hand upon the grave! Instantly the ground opened and the astonished king, peeping in, saw a flight of rough steps, and, at the bottom of them, the fakeer sitting, just as he used to sit, on his rickety bedstead, reading the Koran!

At first the king was so surprised and frightened that he could only stare; but the fakeer beckoned to him to come down, so, mustering up his courage, he boldly stepped down into the grave.

36

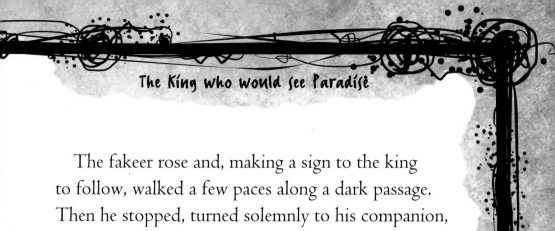

The fakeer rose and, making a sign to the king to follow, walked a few paces along a dark passage. Then he stopped, turned solemnly to his companion, and, with a movement of his hand, drew aside as it were a heavy curtain, and revealed — what? No one knows what was shown to the king, nor did he ever tell anyone; but, when the fakeer at length dropped the curtain, and the king turned to leave the place, he had had his glimpse of Paradise! Trembling in every limb, he staggered back along the passage, and stumbled up the steps out of the tomb into the fresh air again.

The dawn was breaking. It seemed odd to the king that he had been so long in the grave. It appeared but a few minutes ago that he had descended, passed along a few steps to the place where he had peeped beyond the curtain, and returned again after perhaps five minutes of that wonderful view! And what was it he had seen? He racked his brains to remember, but he could not call to mind a single thing! How curious everything looked too! His own city, which by now

he was entering, seemed changed and strange to him! The sun was already up when he turned into the palace gate and entered the hall. It was full; a chamberlain came across and asked him why he sat unbidden in the king's presence. "But I am the king!" he cried.

"What king?" said the chamberlain.

"The true king of this country," said he indignantly.

Then the chamberlain went away, and spoke to the king who sat on the throne, and the old king heard words like "mad," "age," "compassion." Then the king on the throne called him to come forward and, as he went, he caught sight of himself reflected in the polished steel shield of the bodyguard, and he started back in horror! He was old, decrepit, dirty, and ragged! His long white beard and locks were unkempt, and straggled all over his chest and shoulders. Only one sign of royalty remained to him, and that was the signet-ring upon his right hand. He dragged it off with shaking fingers and held it up to the king.

"Tell me who I am," the old king cried; "there is my signet, who once sat where you sit — even yesterday!"

The king looked at him compassionately, and examined the signet with curiosity. Then he commanded, and they brought out dusty records and archives of the kingdom, and old coins of previous reigns, and compared them faithfully. At last the king turned to the old man and said: "Old man, such a king as this whose signet thou hast, reigned seven hundred years ago; but he is said to have disappeared, none know whither; where did you get the ring?"

Then the old man cried and wailed; for he understood that he, who was not content to wait patiently to see the Paradise of the faithful, had been judged already. And he turned and left the hall without a word, and went into the jungle, where he lived for twenty-five years a life of prayer and meditation, until at last the Angel of Death came to him, and mercifully released him, purged and purified through his punishment.